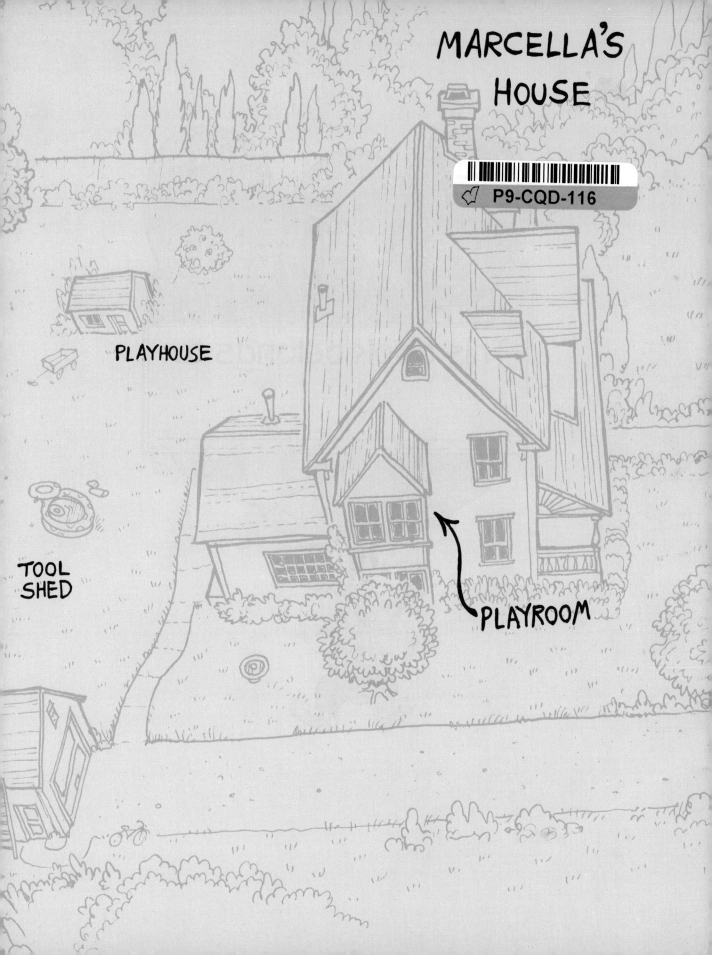

MARCELLA'S
HOUSE

P9-CQD-116

PLAYHOUSE

TOOL
SHED

PLAYROOM

This book belongs to:

_____

Raggedy Ann & Andy's

GROW AND LEARN LIBRARY

VOLUME 3

SAM LAMB MOVES AWAY

A LYNX BOOK

This book is published by Lynx Books, a division of Lynx Communications, Inc., 41 Madison Avenue, New York, New York 10010. The name "Lynx" together with the logotype consisting of a stylized head of a lynx is a trademark of Lynx Communications, Inc.

Raggedy Ann and Andy's Grow-and-Learn Library, the names and depictions of Raggedy Ann, Raggedy Andy and all related characters are trademarks of Macmillan, Inc.

In and out. In and out. Marcella was in and out of the playroom all morning long. She moved all of her favorite games to one side of the room. She rearranged her books very neatly and stacked her blocks.

The dolls who lived in the playroom sat and watched. Something was happening to make Marcella so busy. What could it be?

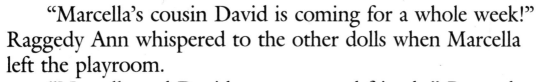

"Marcella's cousin David is coming for a whole week!" Raggedy Ann whispered to the other dolls when Marcella left the playroom.

"Marcella and David are very good friends," Raggedy Andy added. He remembered when Marcella had taken him and Raggedy Ann along when she went to David's home for a vacation.

Brring-brring! The doorbell rang early in the afternoon. David had arrived!

"I'll get it!" shouted Marcella as she ran to the front door. Then Marcella brought David upstairs to the playroom.

Marcella showed David her toys and introduced him to some of the dolls. "This is Percy the Policeman Doll," Marcella told him, "and Bubbles the Clown Doll, Babette the French Doll, and The Camel with the Wrinkled Knees. And here is Sunny Bunny and, of course, you already know Raggedy Ann and Raggedy Andy." Before she could finish introducing everyone, David interrupted.

"I like all of your dolls," David said, "but this one is my favorite!" David picked up Sam Lamb. "I have a little zoo right near my house," he told Marcella. "I go there to pet the baby animals. I like the lambs the most. They look just like this doll."

Marcella and David played with her toys and dolls all afternoon. They built a castle of blocks. Then they put a toy elevator in it and made it go up and down.

They gave rides to the dolls who were little enough to fit.

Finally, it was time for dinner—and then to go to sleep.

After everyone in the house went to bed, the dolls could finally talk about the day.

"Marcella's cousin is very nice," said Sunny Bunny.

"And David certainly does like Sam Lamb," added Greta the Dutch Doll.

"Marcella let David take Sam Lamb to bed with him," Raggedy Ann told them. "I think David misses his own dolls. I'm sure Sam Lamb will make him feel better."

Each day that week, Marcella and David played together.

They went to the playground.

And to the library.

And to a park that had ducks in a pond.

David took Sam Lamb with him everywhere they went.

One night while Marcella and David were having their
dinner, Sam Lamb finally had a chance to tell the others
what he had learned.

"David doesn't live very far from here anymore," he
said. "His family just moved to a new house that is only
about two hours away by car."

Two hours sounded like a very long way to most of the
dolls.

The week passed very quickly. When it was time for David to go home, Marcella knew she would miss her cousin. She decided to give him something very special to help him remember his vacation at her house. Marcella knew that the thing that would be most special to David was something that was very special to her, too.

"Here," she said, carefully handing Sam Lamb to her cousin. "I know you'll take good care of him."

As David left with Sam Lamb, Raggedy Ann and the other dolls watched from the playroom window. They felt very sad to see their friend leave. They knew that what Marcella had done was very nice, but they wished she hadn't done it.

The dolls still felt sad as the days went by.

"I wonder what Sam Lamb is doing," Babette said one night.

"Do you think he ever thinks about us?" asked Sunny Bunny.

"I sure wish we could see him," said Percy.

"Me, too!" the other dolls all agreed.

Raggedy Ann climbed out of her bed and walked over to the window. As she looked out at the stars she thought that perhaps Sam was looking at the same stars. This made Raggedy Ann feel that Sam Lamb was not so very far away. That's when she had an idea.

First she gathered together all the crayons and pencils and paper she could find. Then Raggedy Ann said, "We can write letters to Sam Lamb and tell him that we miss him and that we hope he's happy."

The dolls thought that was a very good idea. Everyone wanted to write a letter to Sam Lamb.

The little dollhouse dolls could barely hold their pencils. There was a lot of mumbling about how to spell some of the hard words. Raggedy Ann told the dolls who couldn't write real words that they should draw pictures for Sam.

"Now for the rest of my plan!" she said. Raggedy Ann asked Raggedy Andy and Bubbles the Clown to help her. "Come on!" she said. "We must visit the Deep Deep Woods."

The three dolls tiptoed out of the playroom. They quietly jumped from one step to the next all the way downstairs. Then they squeezed through the doggie door in the kitchen and scampered down the path toward the Deep Deep Woods.

The moonlight helped light their way. The same stars Raggedy Ann had been watching before were twinkling in the sky above them.

They ran until they met their good friends the
sparrows.

"Can you help us find out where Marcella's cousin
David lives?" Raggedy Ann asked.

"I'm sure we can," the sparrows answered. The
sparrows flew from town to town. They knew that the blue
jays and the robins and their other friends in the nearby
towns would help them.

"When you find out where he lives," Raggedy Andy asked them, "would you come to the playroom and help us with our plan?"

Then Bubbles told the sparrows about the letters they had written.

The sparrows were very happy to help their doll friends.

So the three dolls hurried back to the playroom and collected the letters. Very early the next morning, the sparrows arrived at the playroom windowsill.

They had found David's house and had come back for the letters.

Sam Lamb had thought of his friends back in Marcella's playroom many times. He had made new friends at David's house, but his old friends were still on his mind.

When the sparrows arrived on his windowsill, Sam couldn't believe his eyes. They were carrying so many wonderful letters. He read each one over and over again. And then, with the help of his new friends, he wrote back.

The dolls at Marcella's house thought it was a very long time before they got Sam's answer.

"Do you think he ever got our letters?" asked The Camel with the Wrinkled Knees.

"Maybe he doesn't care about us anymore," Tim the Toy Soldier said sadly.

But when Sam's answer arrived, they knew that wasn't true.

"Dear Everyone!" Sam Lamb wrote. "Thank you for your letters! There is a lot I have to tell you. I have made many new friends, and my new house is very nice. David has taken me to the zoo to see the real lambs. And we've gone to the beach.

"But the most important thing I have to tell you is that I miss you all very much. Please write to me again. Let's stay friends forever."

The letter was signed, "Love, Sam Lamb."

The dolls were so happy.

"Let's write to Sam Lamb again!" Sunny Bunny suggested.

"Great!" said the others.

The letters flew back and forth.

Then came the surprise. Sam Lamb wrote that he and David would be visiting for a weekend.

The dolls were so excited they could scarcely keep from asking Marcella when David and Sam Lamb were coming!

It had been weeks since the dolls had seen Sam Lamb.
And several more days passed before David and Sam Lamb
finally arrived. The dolls had so many things to talk about,
they found it very difficult to wait until David and Marcella
left them alone. But they were all very happy that Sam
Lamb was able to spend the whole night in the playroom.

When it was almost time for David and Sam Lamb to leave, everyone got very sad again.

"We wish you could stay with us forever," they told Sam Lamb.

Then Raggedy Ann put her arm on Sam Lamb's shoulder. "But I'll bet if you did," she said, "you'd miss all your new friends in David's playroom."

Sam Lamb looked at her for a minute and then he said, "I hadn't thought about that, but I would. They are special to me, too."

"We'll always look forward to your visits, Sam Lamb. I hope we'll get to come see you soon, too," Raggedy Andy told him.

And they didn't even have to promise that they'd write to each other. They always did. In the beginning they wrote every day, and then a little less often. But the dolls always thought of Sam Lamb, and he always thought of them.

"You see," Raggedy Ann told them one day, "when your friend moves away, you *can* still be friends forever."

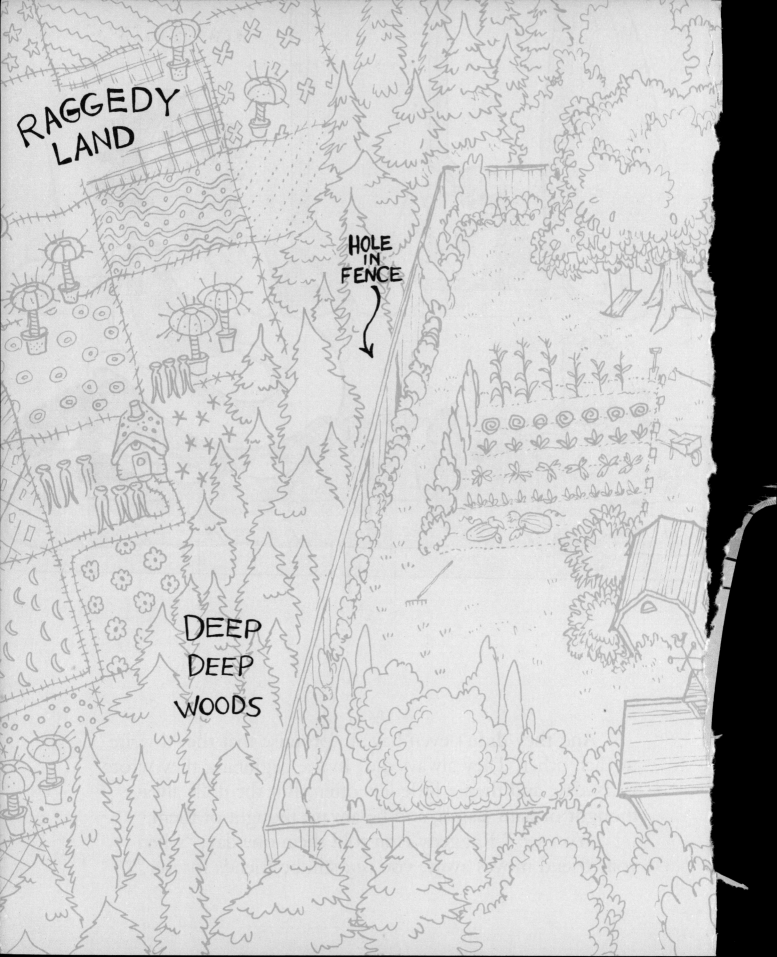